Also by Lynea Bowdish

Living with My Stepfather Is Like Living with a Moose

Pictures by Blanche Sims

Brooklyn, Bugsy, and Me

LYNEA BOWDISH

Brooklyn, Bugsy, and Me

Pictures by Nancy Carpenter

Farrar Straus Giroux   New York

Text copyright © 2000 by Lynea Bowdish
Illustrations copyright © 2000 by Nancy Carpenter
All rights reserved
Distributed in Canada by Douglas & McIntyre Ltd.
Printed in the United States of America
Designed by Filomena Tuosto
First edition, 2000
3   5   7   9   10   8   6   4   2

Library of Congress Cataloging-in-Publication Data
Bowdish, Lynea
    Brooklyn, Bugsy, and me / Lynea Bowdish ; pictures by Nancy
Carpenter — 1st ed.
        p.   cm.
    Summary: In 1953 nine-year-old Sam moves with his mother from West Virginia
to Brooklyn and finds that his grandfather, a well-liked neighborhood character
nicknamed Bugsy, does not seem to want him in his life.
    ISBN 0-374-30993-0
    [1. Brooklyn (New York, N.Y.)—Fiction.   2. Grandfathers—Fiction.
3. Moving, Household—Fiction.]   I. Carpenter, Nancy, ill.   II. Title
PZ7.B67194Br   2000
[Fic]—dc21   99-36267

For two people who are special to this book:

Ronald T. "Ben" Gaus,

who watched over us, and listened, and

Beverly Reingold,

who treats manuscripts and writers with

courtesy, skill, and kindness

Brooklyn, Bugsy, and Me

1

"Don't step on your father," Mom said, pushing the valise farther under the train seat.

As if I would. At nine years old, I knew better. I just wished she had sent him with the moving van, instead of carrying him with us.

Mom always did things differently. For example, we celebrated Christmas Day on New Year's.

Mom was a patient cashier at a hospital. She worked Christmas Day because she got paid extra. So while everyone else was enjoying New Year's, we were opening presents and eating turkey.

When I was a baby, Mom sometimes sang me to sleep. But she didn't sing soft, cuddly lullabies. Mom sang "The Star-Spangled Banner." It was the only song she knew, and she sang it loud. For some reason, it put me to sleep.

What was really different, though, was what she did with Dad. He died in World War II, at the Battle of the Bulge in Belgium. That was in 1944, almost nine years ago. I was just born. I was named Sam, after Dad.

Europe had one of the worst winters ever. It was bad in West Virginia, too, where we lived. The ground in the cemetery was frozen. The Army said they'd bury Dad, but Mom had him cremated. She was half crazy, she told me later, and only went on living because I yelled so loud to be fed.

Mom never got around to burying Dad or scattering his ashes. He wound up in an urn on top of the china closet.

After a while, I got used to her talking to him. "Good morning, Samuel," she'd say. I knew she wasn't talking to me. She called me Sam. Then she'd pat the urn a little.

Or she'd say, "I'm not getting my raise. The hospital doesn't have the money."

Dad was the first to hear the news, good or bad. It was as if he were really sitting there, in a chair, instead of in an urn next to a vase and some candlesticks.

Whenever somebody asked about him, I said he was in the family plot in the cemetery, with bushes and flowers planted around him. It sounded better than the china closet.

"You should have sent him with the moving van," I said.

Mom shrugged. "I was afraid they'd lose him." She leaned over and patted the satchel, as if making sure he was still there.

What we were doing now was different, too. Everyone knew city people wanted to move to the country or, at the very least, to the suburbs. But here we were, on a train from West Virginia heading toward New York City, and we were actually going to live there.

Every time I said New York City, Mom would say, "No, Sam, we're moving to Brooklyn."

As if there were a difference. To me they were both buildings and concrete and dirt and stuffy air, and now, in mid-August, lots of heat. And, of course, gangs waiting on corners to beat me up. The newspapers had articles about them. Juvenile delinquents, they were called. And they all lived in the cities.

West Virginia wasn't like that, at least not our part. It had big mountains, little streams, lots of trees and sky. Even our little house had a stream nearby, and a river not far. My friend Bud and I fished and skipped stones and swam and did every-thing city people wanted to do.

But Mom said moving couldn't be helped. After the war, people started using oil for heat instead of coal. The mines closed down, and people lost jobs. Even the hospital where Mom worked was affected, and she was fired. After three months of not finding a job, she decided we had to live with Gramps.

Gramps was a bit different himself. He was my mother's father, and I'd met him twice. He never came to visit us. Mom said he couldn't leave his dog, Red.

The first time we visited him was six years ago. I was three years old. He picked me up and threw me to the ceiling. I screamed my head off.

I still remember the trip down. It was in slow motion. I knew I'd be flattened against the floor, and it would hurt like blazes. I don't remember him catching me, but he must have, because I didn't wind up with anything broken. I hid from him for the rest of the visit.

The second time we met was two years ago. He gripped my hand so tight I figured I'd never fish again. And I love to fish.

But that year Gramps had bought a television. It was small, a seven-inch, not like the bigger ones in the windows of TV stores. We didn't have TV at home, so I watched it the whole time I was there.

The reception wasn't too good. The picture was a little fuzzy, and it had a lot of static. But I watched *Kukla, Fran, and Ollie,* and *Howdy Doody.* And after Gramps looked at his fifteen-minute news program, we all watched Milton Berle. When Mom and Gramps were in bed, I even watched the test pattern that came on after the stations went off the air.

On that trip, Gramps left me alone. He never tried to talk to me. I didn't even remember what he looked like.

And now we were going to live with him.

"I wish Gramps didn't live in New York," I said.

"Brooklyn, Sam," Mom said. "And it's just for a while. Just until I find a job and we get on our feet. Then we'll go back."

I noticed she didn't say "back home," the way most people would. I thought of it as home. But she didn't.

Mom was from Brooklyn. She met Dad when he was in the Army and on leave. They got married, and she followed him to West Virginia, where he was from. When he returned to the war, she lived with his parents. I was born in the house they rented. Dad's parents died when I was young. Mom and I stayed on in the house.

Now, with Mom's job over, I figured there wasn't much reason for her to rush back. But West Virginia was home to me.

The train ride was boring. At first we saw countryside. Then houses. The closer we got to New York, the more buildings and concrete we saw.

A lot of the buildings still had the presidential election posters stuck to them. Most of them said "I Like Ike," but I saw a few for Stevenson. Mom had voted for General Eisenhower. She didn't blame him for Dad's dying. She said General Eisenhower had helped end the war.

The glare from the afternoon sun highlighted the dirt on the train window. I dozed off, my head against the pane.

The next thing I knew, Mom was pushing me awake. Drool was running down my chin, and my mouth tasted funny. We were in New York. Ycch.

2

Gramps wasn't home when we got there, but Mom had a key. The movers had delivered our stuff, and had wedged it in where they could.

Mom's double bed was set up in what looked like Gramps's junk room. Mom said we'd share the closet. My bed was in a corner of the living room. The movers had piled the boxes in the middle of the room. They had left me a path to the bed.

Mom took a quick look around. Then she dug Dad out of the valise and put him on our china closet.

"We're here, Samuel," she said to the urn, and gave it a pat. "Make yourself at home."

Dad was settled. I hoped it wouldn't be as easy for Mom, or we might never go back.

I made my way through the tunnel of boxes and threw myself on the bed.

The air was stifling. All the windows were open, but nothing stirred. Exhaust fumes came up to the third floor and parked themselves above my head. Sounds drifted up from the street, too—horns honking, kids yelling, brakes squealing.

I'd never heard so much noise. Maybe they were celebrating. It wasn't a holiday. It was only Friday afternoon. Did city people celebrate that?

Mom turned on a floor fan and started unpacking the boxes.

"Here are the candlesticks, Samuel," she said.

I could hear her over the loud hum of the fan.

"And look," she added, "my mother's vase. I'm so glad it didn't get broken in the move."

She rambled on. I looked around for the television. It sat on a small table by the front window. I decided I'd better wait to turn it on until Gramps came home and said I could.

The man who opened the door looked nothing like the old gray-haired man I'd imagined. This man was tall, straight, and thick. He didn't look all that old.

He touched my mother on the shoulder as a hello. I swung my legs off the bed and sat up.

"Hi," I said.

He nodded to me, but didn't say a word to either of us. He sure didn't seem happy to see us.

He leaned over to unleash a brown dog who looked as if he'd gone for a walk that had been three miles too long.

"This is Red," Gramps said. "Don't feed him anything. He's on a special diet for his stomach. And don't come at him from his right. He has trouble seeing from that side."

Red came over, sniffed my foot, and collapsed on the small rug by my bed. In two seconds he was snoring heavily.

Gramps sat down in a soft brown chair that might once have been blue and watched Mom.

"The trip was just fine," Mom said to him, although he hadn't asked. "The packing was a chore, but Sam was a big help. It shouldn't take too long to get these boxes sorted. And next week I'll start job hunting. It's too late today. Besides, I think it's best to do that at the beginning of the week, don't you?"

She didn't notice that Gramps didn't answer. He just sat and listened. Once in a while he nodded.

I could feel myself getting sleepy, and I lay back down. If I were lucky I'd sleep through fourth grade, then right on through high school. I'd wake up in time to move out on my own and go home to West Virginia.

Mom talked all through dinner, while Gramps kept quiet. Afterward, she asked, "Is it okay if Sam looks at television?"

I think she knew I felt uncomfortable asking.

"Needs a new picture tube," Gramps said briefly, not looking at me. "Hasn't worked in a year."

I was doomed. I had nothing to do. My comic books were in the boxes somewhere. I didn't know anyone. I was trapped, and dying of the heat.

Gramps and Mom shared the newspaper. Mom handed me the funnies to read. After a while, they went to bed.

The air cooled down a little. The fan tried to push it around the room. I directed the fan at the bed, and the breeze ruffled the hair on Red's stomach. He looked up at me and wagged once in appreciation. Then he went back to sleep.

My last thought that night was that I'd have to do something about getting myself home. Mom was already crazy enough for both of us. I didn't want to get that way, too.

3

I spent the next week feeling bored. After I
unpacked my comic books and put them under my
bed, I had nothing to do. I knew most of the
Superman comics by heart.

Gramps brought the newspaper home with him
every afternoon. It was called *The Brooklyn Eagle*.
I wondered when was the last time an eagle had
visited Brooklyn.

The funnies weren't bad. But I could read them
only so many times without getting tired of them.

"Go out for a walk," Mom said. "Meet the kids
in the neighborhood."

Yeah, sure. It wasn't like West Virginia, where everyone in town knew everyone else. What would I say to these kids? "You want to be my friend?" I'd probably get slugged. The newspapers were full of articles about juvenile delinquents and gang wars and crime.

I was so bored, I actually offered to help Mom unpack. But the path through the boxes was narrow, and Mom and I kept bumping into each other. "Go read your comics," she said finally.

I got off the bed only to eat meals. From there I watched as, one by one, the boxes in the middle of the room disappeared.

Every morning Gramps went out with Red for a couple of hours. I couldn't understand how Red could walk that long, but I didn't ask. It would sound as if I thought the dog was falling apart. I also didn't ask Gramps where he was going. It seemed pretty clear that he didn't want me along. If he did, he would invite me.

Gramps came home every day for lunch. Mom talked the whole time.

"I'm almost done with the unpacking," Mom said. "I've repacked a lot of things we won't need and piled the boxes in the corner of my room. Everything should be in order by the time I get a job."

Gramps nodded once in a while as Mom rattled on, but mostly he just ate. So did I. If he wasn't going to talk to me, I wasn't going to talk to him.

Every day after lunch, Gramps went out again, but without Red. I couldn't help wondering where he spent all his time. Did old men have girlfriends? What an awful thought.

By Friday Mom had answered some want ads by phone, and had an interview at a hospital on Tuesday of the following week.

Monday morning I woke up to voices. Mom was talking to Gramps at the table. I turned over, but I couldn't help hearing.

"I'm sorry we had to do this, Pop," Mom said. "I know it's crowded. And it can't be easy for you."

"We'll manage," Gramps said.

"But you've been alone so long," Mom said.

"Mama died before Sam was even born. That's a long time to get set in your ways."

Gramps didn't say anything.

"It's hard on Sam, too," Mom said. "He misses fishing and his friends."

"Ummm," Gramps said. And that was the end of the discussion.

Later, after Gramps and Red left, Mom suggested I might want to sit on the stoop. "Gramps and I are going to the grocery store later if you want to join us," she said.

I shuddered. I preferred sitting on the stoop. But I just said, "No thanks."

In West Virginia, we didn't have stoops. We had porches or back steps or front steps, but we didn't have stoops. So when Mom said I should sit on the stoop for a while, I figured the suggestion had come from Gramps.

Outside, I closed my eyes really tight. Maybe the city would disappear. But I could still smell the automobile fumes and hear the horns honk and feel the hot, heavy air that never moved.

"Hey!"

The voice must have been directed at me, because it spoke again.

"Hey!"

A skinny little kid stood on the sidewalk, his hands stuffed in his pockets. His eyes squinted against the afternoon sun. He was sweating, and I could see a line of dirt where his chin met his neck.

"I'm Tony," he said. "You're new here."

I couldn't argue with that, so I didn't say anything.

Tony sat down next to me. He took a little red box out of his pocket, dumped sunflower seeds into his hand, and offered me some. I shook my head.

"I hear you're going into fourth grade in the fall. That's great. We'll be in the same class. We're having Mr. Harris. He's a real pain. Lots of homework. Lots of grammar. You're Sam."

I couldn't argue with that, either. I wondered how he knew about me. I also wondered how he

could talk so fast. He popped a sunflower seed into his mouth and started to suck on it.

"I'm from West Virginia," I said. "We're not staying here long."

"Your mom has an appointment for a job tomorrow," Tony said. "I hope she gets it. That'd be great."

He cracked the seed with his teeth and ate the nut, all without using his hands. Then he spat the shells into his hand and popped another seed into his mouth.

"My father works in the city," Tony said.

I tried to look as if I knew what he meant.

"You know," he said. "New York. The city."

I nodded.

"How do you know so much about us?" I asked.

Tony shrugged. "People talk. Bugsy tells his friends and they tell other people. Sooner or later, I hear it. It's interesting. Don't you think people are interesting?"

He paused for a breath. It was amazing that he ever heard anything. All he had done since sitting down was talk. And chew.

"Sure you won't have some?" Tony said, popping another seed into his mouth. "Two cents a box at Moe's. They're great."

I shook my head again. I was going to ask about Moe's, but he kept talking.

"Bugsy says you read comics all the time," Tony said. "He said maybe I should come over and meet you. He thinks you ought to get out more."

"Nice of him," I said. I hoped Tony could hear the sarcasm. "Who's Bugsy, anyway?"

Tony turned around and stared at me. "Who's Bugsy? Why, the guy you're living with."

I was a blank.

"Bugsy," Tony said again. "Your grandfather."

I almost fell off the steps. "My grandfather's name is Bugsy?"

Tony nodded.

This kid had to be confused. I didn't have a grandfather named Bugsy. Did I?

4

I stared at Tony. "You must be thinking of some-one else," I said.

Tony laughed. "That's what everyone calls him," he said. "Bugsy's been in the neighborhood longer than anyone. He lives here, on the third floor. His daughter and grandson have moved in from West Virginia. That's you."

I couldn't believe it. My silent, cold, unfriendly grandfather had a nickname. And the nickname was "Bugsy." Like some gangster. Or a movie cartoon character.

"It couldn't be the same guy," I said.

Tony shrugged again. He got off the stoop and started kicking at a crack in the sidewalk. "Suit yourself. Want to play stoopball?"

There was even a game named after these stupid steps.

"Maybe some other time," I said. I didn't want to tell him I didn't know how to play stoopball.

"What do you like to do?" Tony asked.

I joined Tony on the sidewalk. His eyes stopped squinting, and I could see they were brown and bright. Happy eyes, my mother would call them. Eyes that looked at you and liked what they saw, whatever it was.

"I like hiking the mountains," I said.

"No mountains here," Tony said. "What else?"

"At home I swim in the river," I said. "Bud and I rig up a rope. We swing out on it over the water. Then we let go."

"Sounds great," Tony said. "Nothing like that around here."

"Fishing's my favorite thing," I said. "I love to fish. My father used to fish."

"Did you fish together?" Tony asked.

"I don't remember my father," I said. "But I fish a lot, just like he did."

I looked at all the concrete around me. "I mean, I used to fish," I added.

"I like stoopball," Tony said. "And the school-yard isn't far, if you want some basketball. And *War of the Worlds* is coming to the movies next week. I've already seen *It Came from Outer Space*. That's in 3-D. Great. And there's always stickball."

"We played softball at school," I said.

"Stickball's not really the same," Tony said. "You play with a stick, not a bat. There's no pitcher. And the rules are different. We play in the street. You have to watch out for cars, though. When the traffic's bad, we post lookouts. But this is a one-way street, so that helps."

For the first time, I noticed that the cars on the street were all going in the same direction. Still, dodging them in order to play ball didn't sound too safe.

"We use the fire hydrant and manhole covers for bases," Tony said. "And the sewer."

I looked at Tony. He pointed to where the sidewalk went down a step onto the street.

"That's the gutter," Tony said. "It runs to the sewer, that metal grating near the corner. Sometimes you can find money and stuff down there. But it's hard to get it out. You need string and a hook to pull it up. Some kids use gum, but the stuff doesn't always stick. It's great when you find something."

He finally took a breath. "Anyway, next time we play stickball, you should play," he said. "It's great."

Evidently Tony thought everything was great. Even the city.

"Does the traffic ever stop?" I asked.

Tony shrugged again. "Sunday mornings, and around suppertime, and real late," he said. "That's the best time in the summer, because the heat goes down. Maybe we can get a game up tonight."

"I don't think so," I said. "I've been helping my mother unpack."

The lie didn't sit well. But I felt funny telling Tony I wasn't good at ball playing.

"Too bad." Tony shrugged. "Bugsy plays with us sometimes. Everybody wants to be on his team. His team usually wins."

I was speechless. Gramps played stickball? With a bunch of little kids? I thought he didn't like kids. Maybe it was just me he didn't like.

"Gotta go," Tony said suddenly. "I have to babysit my sister while my mother goes to the grocery store."

Tony dumped a handful of shells in the garbage can next to the stoop.

"I live down the block, on the corner, over the butcher's," he said. "Come on. I'll show you."

We walked to the corner.

"That's where we live," Tony said. He pointed across the street to the butcher's. On the floor above, I could see curtains pulled back from the open windows.

"It's great," Tony said. "The trolley stops right out front."

This time I knew what Tony was talking about. Mom and I had taken the subway and the trolley when we got off the train.

"Gotta go," Tony said. "See you."

With a wave, he ran off. I watched as he crossed the street and ducked into a doorway at the side of the store.

I went back to the stoop and sat down again on the steps. I didn't know people lived over stores. And I didn't know streets were called blocks here. At home, we called everything roads.

I'd never get used to this place. And I didn't really want to.

The ants now decided I was part of the stoop. They were crawling all over my shorts. I let them. It was good to see something that reminded me of home.

Bugsy. Gramps. Was it possible?

5

I didn't think spying on Gramps was illegal or immoral. Still, it didn't seem right. But what if I happened to be out at the same time? And didn't have anything else to do? And happened to go in the same direction? That wouldn't hurt anyone.

So the next morning I decided to be out at the same time as Gramps. "I'm going for a walk," I told Mom.

Gramps was hooking the leash onto Red. I wanted to get downstairs before he did. Mom's face lit up. I guess she was glad to see me off the bed. "Don't go too far," she said.

I raced downstairs and up to the corner. I crossed at the light, and then crossed again. I didn't want to stand in front of the butcher's. I might run into Tony. Instead, I stood near a tiny shoe-repair store, way back from the curb, and watched for Gramps.

A few minutes later, he and Red came out of the apartment house. Red led the way. He stopped at most light poles and lifted his leg. Gramps didn't hurry him along.

They were easy to follow because they walked so slowly. That gave me plenty of time to feel guilty about what I was doing. I should have asked Gramps if I could tag along. But since we never talked, it was hard to start up that kind of conversation. Besides, I felt that he didn't want me.

Gramps and Red turned a couple of corners. They came to a tiny park at the edge of a small group of buildings. All it had were a couple of trees and some benches. At least it was green.

The heat had already settled in for the day. Most of the prime spots in the shade had been taken. Old women in beat-up lawn chairs crowded together to talk. Two women sat on the grass next to strollers and played with their babies. A group of men huddled around a game board set up on a bench.

I watched as Gramps approached. I couldn't hear the people, but I could tell they all knew him. He moved from group to group. Hands reached out to shake his, and to rub Red. They all rubbed him on his left side. There was lots of laughter.

Gramps finally settled down on a bench, where it looked as if a spot had been saved. Red lay by his feet and curled into a ball. So much for the two-hour walk I thought he got every morning.

I stood watching for a while. Then a police car drove by, and the cop glanced at me. He probably thought I was a juvenile delinquent, hanging around, looking for trouble. That was all I needed,

to be picked up for loitering. I turned around and started off quickly, as if I suddenly remembered I had to be somewhere.

I soon realized I was lost. None of the buildings looked familiar. I walked back to the corner, but it didn't look familiar either. The park had disappeared.

In the woods at home, this never would have happened. I knew every tree and branch. When I hiked into new territory, I was careful to mark the way. My mother had read me *Hansel and Gretel* when I was little. I knew about the bread crumbs.

So I just stood there. A nine-year-old boy from West Virginia doesn't stand in the middle of New York, or Brooklyn even, and scream his head off. But I sure wanted to.

"Hey!"

Through the traffic and people noise, the shouted word felt like a life jacket.

"Hey, Sam!"

The voice was louder now, if that was possible.

There was movement among the people around

me, and Tony appeared. "I thought that was you," he said, panting from his run. "Where're you going?"

I couldn't think of a good answer. I'm lost and I'm going to die here on this corner unless someone gets me home didn't seem right. But I could feel my breath return and my face cool down.

"Just looking around," I said. "Getting to know the area."

"I'm heading home," Tony said. "My mom wanted some rolls from the bakery."

I noticed the brown bag he carried.

"I'd better go," he said. "Mom wants these for lunch. See you later."

"No!" I yelled, and grabbed his shirt. "I'm heading home, too," I said. "I'll go with you."

It wasn't hard to let him lead. He walked fast, so whenever we had to choose direction, I let him move first.

This time I marked the way. Water Street (no water that I could see) to the cleaners on the corner of Water and Watson. Cross Water and walk two blocks on Watson to Greeley, passing a store that sold all kinds of junk. A right, one block on Greeley, and a left by the fish store.

Tony stopped in front of a butcher shop. "Your place is over there," he said, pointing.

Then I understood. We were in front of his building. And he knew what had happened.

I fumbled for something to say, but he didn't give me a chance. "How about if I call for you after lunch?" he said. "We can go over to the schoolyard and see who's around."

"Sure," I said, trying not to show how embarrassed I was about getting lost. I wondered how he knew Gramps's phone number.

Tony gave me a light punch on the arm and disappeared through the door next to the butcher shop. When he opened the door, I could see stairs going up.

He sure was quick for a little guy. He was like a deer in the mountains. I'd come across one, and it would hold still for a minute; the next thing, it'd be gone.

I crossed at the light and headed for my spot on the stoop of Gramps's building. The sun was getting hotter and the air heavier. I felt miserable. I'd never learn how to live in this place. My first day out and I had gotten lost.

And I had secretly followed my own grandfather. Already this place was having a bad effect on me. If I stayed here too long, I'd wind up a juvenile delinquent.

A while later, a dog sniffed my feet. It was Red, with Gramps at the other end of the leash. I put my hand out, and Red snarled. This, from the same dog who slept on the rug next to my bed and shared the fan.

"Wrong side," Gramps snapped. "He can't see your hand, but he knows something's coming at him. Watch it, or he'll bite you."

I pulled back. "Sorry," I said.

They climbed the steps slowly. Tony had to be wrong. This man couldn't play stickball with the kids and be called "Bugsy" and be known by everyone in the neighborhood.

But I had seen the people in the park welcome him. I had seen him smile and laugh.

And then I knew what it must be. Gramps didn't want me here. He didn't want me taking up space in his living room, and reading his newspaper, and touching his dog. He didn't want me in his life at all.

6

Tony came by after lunch. Evidently "call for" was different from "call." He didn't mean by phone. He meant in person.

"Hey, Sam."

Tony's voice came up from the street as if he were standing on the fire escape outside the window. For a little guy, he sure had a loud voice.

I went to the window.

"Be right there," I called down.

"Gramps says Tony's a nice boy," Mom said.

As usual, Gramps had gone out after lunch

without Red. He had probably gone back to the park, to be with all those people he liked.

"Tony's okay," I said. "Not like Bud."

"I know you miss Bud," Mom said. "But as long as we're here, you might as well try to make friends."

"I don't understand half of what Tony's talking about," I said. "And I miss fishing."

Mom sighed. "I know. You've always loved fishing. Just like your father."

She looked up at the urn. "Your father loved the mountains. I wonder if he minds being in Brooklyn."

I didn't think he cared much.

"We're going over to the school," I said, changing the subject.

"That's nice. Don't forget that I have my job interview this afternoon."

I nodded. "Good luck."

Part of me didn't mean it. If Mom didn't get the job, maybe she'd rethink going home.

As I left, I heard her talking to Dad. "I'm nervous, Samuel," she said. "But I have a chance at this job, don't you think?"

I didn't wait around to see if he answered her.

Downstairs, Tony was throwing a ball against the stoop.

"Stoopball?" I asked.

"I'm the best around," he said. "I'll show you how to play sometime."

So he knew I couldn't play stoopball. How did he know all these things? Maybe Gramps had told him. And maybe Gramps had told Tony to pay attention to me. The more time I spent with Tony, the less time I'd spend in the apartment. Then Gramps wouldn't have to go out so much.

Tony crammed the ball into his pocket and started down the block. We passed some little girls playing hopscotch on the sidewalk.

"That's my sister," Tony said. "The one with the ponytail. She's nuts about potsy. They play it all day, every day." He shrugged. "Kids."

I had never heard hopscotch called potsy before.

Tony ducked into a small opening between two buildings. "This alley is a shortcut," he explained.

The alley was narrow and dark, and it muffled the street noises. We edged around some empty garbage cans that smelled like oranges. At the other end, we came out on the next street.

"If anyone from the Gang bothers us in the schoolyard, just let me handle it," Tony said.

A quiver started in my gut. "What gang?" I asked.

"The Gang. That's what they call themselves."

Tony walked quickly. I had a hard time keeping up with him, especially in that heat.

"What do they do?" I asked.

"What do you mean?"

"Do they steal cars or beat up old ladies or have gang wars?"

"It's not that kind of gang," Tony said. "They hang around the schoolyard. They pick on little kids. Things like that."

"But the newspapers say gangs fight other gangs and commit crimes," I said. "And the leaders meet to talk about gang wars. They're juvenile delinquents."

"My mom would kill Jimmy if she thought he was a juvenile delinquent," Tony said.

"Who's Jimmy?" I asked.

"My older brother," Tony said impatiently. "He's the leader. He's in high school."

Now I was totally confused. "You mean your brother is the leader of this gang and you're afraid of it?"

"I didn't say I was afraid of it," Tony said. "I just said let me handle it if they pick on you. Besides, Jimmy likes Bugsy. He helped Jimmy out when Jimmy was in a jam."

I didn't understand. As usual.

The schoolyard was a big piece of concrete surrounded by a rusty chain-link fence. The gate hung by broken hinges. I bet it hadn't closed in years. The basketball hoop at the end of the schoolyard had no net.

Tony took me over to a group of kids our age. They were bouncing a ball around. I couldn't catch all their names. Most of them seemed to be going into fourth grade in the fall, and they all complained about Mr. Harris.

"My sister had so much homework last year, she never left the house," Tank, a big kid, said.

"He fails half the class," added another boy. "If you fail, you get him again next year."

"And he belches," said someone else. "After lunch is the worst. Once he belched five times in a row."

That was something to look forward to, I thought.

A group of taller kids sauntered over. Tony's friends moved away.

Those kids had to be in high school. They wore their dungarees low around their hips, with thick leather belts. The sleeves of their T-shirts were rolled up to their shoulders. Across their chests, they had written THE GANG in black.

"Who's this?" one said.

The last G on his shirt was under his left arm. With all that chest to work with, he could have done a better job of getting the name on his shirt.

He came over to me and stood about an inch away. His breath was hot on my face. Part of his lunch must have been onions.

"This is Sam," Tony said, stepping up. "I told you about him, Jimmy. Sam, this is my brother."

"Hi," I said.

Jimmy sneered.

It was about to happen, I thought. I was going to get picked on and maybe beaten up by a gang that didn't even have a name.

7

Jimmy didn't say anything. He just stared at me. Then he stuck out a grimy finger and poked my shoulder. "Rule number one," he said. "Stay out of our way when we want to use the basketball hoop."

He poked my shoulder again. "Rule number two. Stay out of our way when we're in the schoolyard."

I could feel the spot turning black and blue. I hoped there weren't a lot more rules.

He poked again. "Rule number three," he said. "Stay out of our way."

Tony tugged on his brother's T-shirt. "I told you about Sam," Tony said. "Bugsy is his grandfather."

Jimmy stepped back, and his body seemed to loosen up and relax. "Hey, gang, this is Bugsy's grandson," he said to the others.

They looked at me and nodded, as if being related to Gramps were some kind of passport.

Jimmy turned back to me. "Just make sure you follow the rules," he said.

Then, together, Jimmy and the Gang walked over to the school entrance. Jimmy put his foot up on a bench, and they all started pushing one another and laughing.

"That's it?" I said.

"What'd you expect?" Tony said.

I expected to be going home with various broken bones. But I didn't tell him that.

"The next time you bunk into them, just stay out of their way," Tony said.

I could guess what "bunk into" meant—something like run into.

Tony walked me around the outside of the

school and showed me the entrance we had to use. "But I'll be with you," he said. "I know where the classroom is, too. You won't have any trouble."

As we walked home, Tony was careful to point out signposts along the way. First was the cleaners, where a tailor would take your pants up or down if your mother couldn't do it. On the next block was a bar, a men's clothing store, and a candy store.

"That's Moe's, where I buy my sunflower seeds," Tony said. He dipped into his pocket, took out the red box, and popped one into his mouth. "They make the best egg creams in Brooklyn."

I gave Tony a funny look. I didn't even have to ask the question.

"An egg cream," he said. "Seltzer and milk and chocolate mixed together. Great."

So we stopped. The store was cool and dark, and smelled of tobacco. Newspapers and magazines and comic books covered wooden racks and benches at the front. Across from them was a counter with candy bars, strips of paper with colored dots of candy, and boxes of sunflower seeds and pumpkin seeds. A little farther back was a soda fountain.

We climbed up onto stools, and Tony introduced me to the man behind the counter. "Moe, this is Sam," Tony said. "Bugsy's grandson."

"I heard you were here," Moe said.

I wouldn't have been surprised to find out our arrival had been announced in *The Brooklyn Eagle*.

"Bugsy's helped me out a few times," Moe said. "Don't you go giving him any trouble."

Not me, I thought. If I did, I'd have the whole neighborhood to answer to. Everyone around here was nuts about Gramps, although for the life of me, I couldn't see why.

I watched as Moe made the egg cream Tony ordered. No eggs, no cream—just some chocolate syrup, milk, and clear soda from a spigot.

"That's the seltzer," Tony explained.

Tony shared the egg cream with me. It cost eight cents. I didn't have any money, and Tony

had only enough for one. I had to admit, it was pretty good.

When I got home later that afternoon, Mom had big news. She had gotten the job at the hospital. They wanted her to start work in two weeks, the day after Labor Day.

"I know it's in the city," Mom said, "but it's only a block from the subway entrance. And I've always been able to read on the subway."

I sighed. Mom didn't seem to have any problem at all with the language. She knew exactly what "stoop" meant, and "block" and "city." She even knew how to use the subway. She had forgotten all about West Virginia.

For dinner she made macaroni and cheese, my favorite. "A real celebration," she said.

Mom talked up a storm while we ate. After she got her first paycheck, she was going to buy some new clothes. "And we can start up your allowance again," she added.

"That's good," I said, thinking of the egg cream Tony had paid for.

Gramps looked at me, then back at Mom. "I didn't realize . . ."

Mom didn't seem to hear him. "The woman who interviewed me went to the same high school I did," she said. "Imagine that. And next week I'm going with Tony's mom to play bingo at the Catholic church," she added.

I dropped my fork. "You know Tony's mom?"

"When Gramps and I went to the grocery store yesterday," Mom said, "Tony's mother was there. Gramps introduced me. She called me today to see if I wanted to play."

"And you do?" I said.

She glanced up at the urn on the china closet and was quiet for a minute. "It'll be a good way to meet people," she said finally.

I couldn't think of a thing to say. My mother wanted to talk to real people? People who were alive? I thought Dad was all she needed.

Gramps glanced at me, but he didn't say anything, either.

After dinner I heard Mom telling Dad about

her new job while she cleaned up the table. It surprised me. She used to tell Dad everything first.

I went outside and sat on the stoop. Tony's little sister and her friends were down the street playing hopscotch—potsy—whatever.

I wasn't happy about Mom's job. Sure, it meant some money for the first time in a long while. But if it worked out, maybe she wouldn't want to go back to West Virginia.

I wasn't happy about bingo, either. Mom didn't need to meet people. She had Dad and Gramps and me. And if we were leaving soon, she didn't need to have fun.

What if Mom actually liked her job and earned money and made friends here? We might never get home.

8

I was having this awful nightmare. I was swinging out over the river on the rope. Bud kept yelling, "Let go," but I couldn't. So I went on swinging. I was stuck forever.

I rolled over, stretching and groaning, and felt something under the edge of my pillow. It was a quarter. I couldn't believe it. I hadn't seen a quarter in months.

I guessed Mom was celebrating her first paycheck early. Now I could pay for the next egg cream at Moe's.

Mom and Gramps had gone out, probably to the store. Red was asleep on the little rug. I had the place to myself. I wandered around. I happened to glance up at Dad's urn. It looked different.

I took it down from the china closet. Then I noticed what was different: it was dusty. Mom had always kept it shining.

I took the edge of my T-shirt and began cleaning the urn. I wished I'd had a chance to get to know my father.

Mom told me once that after my father died, she cried a lot. She'd sit and hold me and I'd cry along with her. Then she'd sing "The Star-Spangled Banner," and we'd both fall asleep.

Mom always talked about Dad's fishing. Maybe that was why I became interested in it. It was something we would have done together if he had lived. When I went fishing, I felt closer to him.

I spent a long time polishing that urn. It occurred to me that Dad wasn't in West Virginia any more than I was. And he wasn't in the urn, either. We were carrying him with us, wherever we went.

It was a good thing Mom and Gramps came in then or I would have gotten sentimental. I had just enough time to put the urn back. Mom didn't notice, but Gramps caught my eye.

I looked away. "I was just straightening up a little," I said to him, embarrassed.

He didn't say anything. He woke up Red, and they headed out for a walk. Mom started unpacking a grocery bag.

"Thanks for the money," I said.

"What money?" she asked.

"You didn't leave me any money?"

"No," she said. "Listen, put the milk away before it goes bad in this heat."

Gramps must have left me the quarter. But why? He didn't like me. Why would he leave me money? Nothing made sense anymore.

I knew I had to thank Gramps, but I dreaded it. That night, while Mom was cleaning up the

kitchen, I took a deep breath. "Thanks, Gramps," I said.

He looked up from the newspaper. "For what?"

He sure wasn't making this easy.

"For the money," I said.

"Oh," he said.

He seemed embarrassed, too. He went back to reading.

So much for that. Why had I bothered?

Tony and I spent the next few days not doing much of anything. We didn't have enough money for the movies, so we listened to the Dodgers games on the radio and read comic books.

We also wandered around the neighborhood. Tony explained who lived where and what they were like. He knew everyone. I realized that if I stayed within a few blocks of the apartment, I wasn't going to get lost again.

While Tony talked, he ate sunflower seeds, and sometimes I chewed one to keep him company. Before long I could crack the shells with my teeth and eat the nuts without using my hands.

The next time we went to Moe's, I paid for two egg creams. I also bought a box of sunflower seeds for each of us.

Mom went to church on Sunday. She said I didn't have to go until Sunday school started the week after Labor Day.

On Tuesday afternoon, Tony bellowed through the front windows. I ran downstairs.

The building across the street was just starting to shade the stoop in front of the apartment house. We sat on the bottom step.

"Bugsy has a surprise for you," Tony said.

"What is it?" I asked.

"I promised him I'd keep it a secret," Tony said.

It sounded as if Gramps and Tony spent a lot of time talking about me. That was beginning to annoy me. And the thought of a surprise made me nervous.

"It'll be tomorrow," Tony said. "And I get to come along."

Gramps didn't say anything that night about the surprise, and I certainly wasn't going to bring it up. But the next morning, when he and Red went for their walk, Mom talked about it. "Gramps thinks you should get out more," she said. "So he has a treat for you. You're supposed to be ready to leave at four o'clock this afternoon.

"And wear your bathing suit," she added.

There wasn't any water around that I could see. Was he going to make me swim somewhere? Like Europe?

"Where are we going?" I asked.

Mom laughed. "Not me," she said. "Just you and Tony and Gramps. And I'm not supposed to tell you where you're going."

I decided I didn't like surprises, and I especially wasn't going to like this one.

9

Tony showed up promptly at four and shouted toward the window.

Mom had packed a big bag of sandwiches and fruit and a thermos of milk. Gramps and I went down.

"Hey, Sam. Hey, Bugsy," Tony said.

"Hey, Tony," Gramps said.

It sounded odd to hear Gramps called "Bugsy." But Tony did it as if he'd been doing it forever. Most likely he had.

We started walking, and I followed along behind. It was just as well. Tony smelled a little, as if he hadn't taken a bath or something. This way the smell wasn't too bad.

Tony talked the whole time, about Mr. Harris and the Gang and how happy his mother was that the Korean War had ended. Jimmy would be old enough for the Army when he graduated this year, and now he wouldn't have to fight. Jimmy was disappointed. Gramps listened, as usual, and said a word or two once in a while, but Tony did most of the talking.

We had gone about three blocks when Gramps stopped in front of a small house. It had a garage attached. Gramps took out a key ring. When he found the one he was looking for, he unlocked the garage door. Inside was an old Packard.

Tony acted as if nothing was wrong, but I couldn't figure it out. Did Gramps own the house? Had someone said he could use the car?

High on the inside wall of the garage was a shelf. Gramps took down two poles.

"Bugsy said we can share," Tony said to me. "I don't have my own fishing pole."

They looked like fishing poles, all right. But

they couldn't be. There was no river around. I must have looked confused, because Tony laughed.

"The secret's out," he said. "We're going fishing. It was Bugsy's idea. To make you feel more at home."

"We're going fishing?" I asked Tony. "But where?"

"At the beach," Tony said.

"What's at the beach?" I said.

Tony laughed. "The ocean, of course," he said. "We're going night fishing. At Riis Park."

There was an ocean at a park?

Gramps was loading everything into the trunk.

"You mean Gramps has a boat?" I asked Tony.

He laughed again. "We fish from the beach. Casting. Not the kind of fishing you know."

It sure wasn't. At home, I'd sit on a rock overhanging the river and drop a line into the water. How could anyone fish from the sand?

Tony took a soggy package out of his pocket and put it in the trunk. "It's squid," he said to me. "For bait. I got it at the fish store."

No wonder Tony smelled. Didn't they use worms? Then again, without dirt you can't have worms. So far, I hadn't seen much dirt in Brooklyn, other than what settled on the tops of cars and in the gutters.

"Does he own this house?" I whispered.

"Of course not," Tony said. "He rents the garage. You know, to keep his car in."

I'd heard of renting a room in a house. But never a garage. I didn't even know Gramps had a car.

Tony jumped into the back, and I got in next to Gramps.

"This is great," said Tony.

Tony chattered the whole way. I stared out the window. For a while, we passed apartments and tall buildings. Then low houses replaced them.

We came to a bridge and stopped to pay the toll. On each side were marsh grasses and sand dunes and water.

At the other end of the bridge, we pulled into a parking field. It was crowded, even this late in the day. We had to walk a long way across the concrete. Even the beach had concrete, I thought.

When we got onto the wooden boardwalk, I stopped. Across a wide stretch of sand was the ocean.

The cool breeze hit my face and dried the sweat. The air smelled of salt and water. The sand was dotted with beach umbrellas. In the distance, waves crashed onto the shore in swirls of white foam. The open space made me dizzy.

"Isn't it great?" Tony asked. "Come on, I'll race you."

Tony took off, and I ran after him. I couldn't help laughing as I stumbled along the sand with the gear. I hadn't felt this free in weeks.

When Gramps caught up with us, we spread out a blanket to sit on. We stripped down to our bathing suits. Even Gramps. His bony legs sticking out of his baggy suit looked just like mine.

"Don't go out beyond the breakers," Gramps called as we raced to the water's edge.

"What does he mean?" I shouted to Tony over the roar of the ocean.

"See where the big waves are crashing, almost in a straight line?" Tony shouted back. "They can pull you out too far."

The water felt cold after the afternoon heat, and was a lot different from the river. It was noisy and choppy. The sand tugged at my feet, pulling them from under me when the waves washed back out. The water tasted salty.

A big wave hit me on the chest. It hurt, and I struggled to stay upright.

Gramps came wading in. "Watch me!" he called out.

When a big wave approached, Gramps turned his side to it, put his arm up, and jumped. He rode right over the top.

I kept watching Gramps; when he jumped, I jumped. Soon I got the rhythm and realized it was easy.

When Gramps saw I knew how to do it, he went back to the beach.

After a while, Gramps called us to eat.

Getting out of the water wasn't as easy as getting in. The sand kept pulling at my feet. But I finally kept them under me and made it to shore.

Sand stuck to my feet and ankles.

"When it dries, you'll be able to brush it off," Gramps said.

As we ate, Tony talked about how great everything was. I didn't say much. Neither did Gramps.

I still had no idea how I was going to fish in the ocean.

10

By the time we'd finished eating, the beach was nearly empty. The sun set quickly once it reached the horizon. The sky turned purple and red and blue and pink, then darkened. Up and down the shoreline, fishermen began setting up their poles.

Gramps opened the package of bait. He started cutting up the squid. It was gray and slimy-looking, and the pieces slid in his hands. It was no worse than worms. At least I'd be able to bait my own hook.

Tony and Gramps went first. I said I wanted to let my food settle and brush off the dry sand. I really wanted to watch them to see if I could learn something. I'd get the chance to make a fool of myself soon enough.

Gramps and Tony walked down to the edge of the water and baited their hooks. I watched Gramps closely. He brought the top of the pole back over his shoulder. Then he flicked the pole forward, and the weighted line sailed out to the water.

Tony fished for a while. From time to time he'd reel the line in to check his bait, replacing it when something took it. Then he came back and handed me the pole. "Maybe you'll have more luck than I did," he said. "It's great, though."

I headed down to the water's edge and stood next to Gramps. I baited the hook. Then I tipped the pole back over my shoulder and flung it forward toward the water.

The line didn't go far. It swung out and back, and hit me in the chest.

Gramps stuck his pole in the sand and came over.

"You have to release the lock on the reel," he said.

He showed me the lock. Then he showed me how to keep my thumb on the unlocked reel and flick the pole forward so that the line flew out to the water. He reeled the line slowly back in, keeping his thumb on it, waiting for the tug that would mean a fish had taken the bait.

I tried it a couple of times. Gramps kept saying, "Good. Steady now. Not so fast. Easy. Good." It was more than I had heard him say since we'd moved to Brooklyn.

He watched me for a few minutes, to see that I had it right.

"You fish like your father," Gramps said suddenly. "He was pretty good at this, too."

"My father?" I couldn't believe it. "I never knew my father fished here."

"When he and your mother first met," Gramps said. "We came down here a couple of times.

Before they moved to West Virginia. I had to show him how to do it, but he caught on fast, just like you."

I had never pictured my father in Brooklyn. It was a nice feeling, knowing he had been here, fishing the way Gramps and I were.

This was certainly different from dropping a line in the river. But the excitement of waiting for a strike was the same.

Soon the only light came from the boardwalk behind us, and from the moon. Gramps caught two fish, and Tony took another turn, but didn't catch anything. When it was my turn again, Gramps didn't even watch me.

Before long I found myself in a rhythm—swing back, flip, reel in; swing back, flip, reel in. I was so hypnotized that I didn't realize my pole was bending toward the water and the line was running out.

"You've got something!" Tony yelled, just as I felt the line moving out under my thumb.

"Let him run with the line!" Gramps shouted. "Then start reeling!"

I dug my heels into the sand, held on to the pole as tight as I could, and let the fish have the line.

By then Gramps and Tony were next to me.

"Now pull," Gramps said.

I brought the pole back over my head a little, pulling the fish toward shore. Then I tipped the pole forward and wound the reel the way Gramps had.

I kept doing it, a little at a time.

Soon the big fish flapped in the shallow water, sparkling in the light from the moon.

"What kind of fish is it, Gramps?" I asked.

"It's called a fluke," Gramps said. "And it's a beauty."

Tony hit me on the back a lot, saying, "Great, great."

We put the fish in Gramps's pail, then stretched out on the sand before starting home.

I crossed my hands under my head and counted the stars. There weren't as many as I used to see in West Virginia. But at least they were there.

"Hey, Sam," Tony said. "What do you think?"

"Great," I said. "Different, but great."

We were silent for a while, and after a few minutes, Tony's breathing changed. He was asleep.

I took a deep breath. It was now or never.

"Gramps?" I said.

"Yeah, Sam," Gramps said.

"Why do people call you Bugsy?"

Gramps laughed softly. "Your grandmother started that," Gramps said. "She always said I had big ears. She began calling me Bugs—like the rabbit. Soon it got changed to Bugsy. It's been that ever since."

I didn't understand. Gramps didn't have big ears. If anything, he had small ones, like mine, flat to his head.

Then, suddenly, I knew. Gramps had big ears, all right. He was always listening to people: to what they thought about and cared about and worried about. He was too busy listening to talk much. But that didn't mean he didn't like me.

Bugsy. My grandmother had been right. The name suited him just fine.

11

The next morning I made a big decision. Gramps and Red were getting ready to leave for the park.

"Gramps?" I said, my voice cracking a little.

"Umm," he answered, hooking Red's leash.

"Would it be okay if I went for a walk with you?" I asked.

He smiled. "Sure. We're going over to the park. People have been wanting to meet my family. I thought you'd never ask."

So that was it! Gramps had thought I wasn't interested.

When we got to the park, Gramps introduced me to everyone. They welcomed me, and made jokes and laughed and called him Bugsy.

I noticed that Gramps listened to them all. They told him their troubles, and what was going on. He didn't seem to mind. He smiled and nodded. He even smiled at me once. I found myself smiling back. He really did have big ears.

That night Tony called for me to play stickball. "And tell Bugsy we need another guy," he added at the top of his voice.

I told Gramps about the game. Then I ran down the stairs.

Outside, dusk had settled in and traffic had calmed down. The air had cooled off a bit; something in it signaled the start of school and the coming of fall.

Gramps joined us a few minutes later. Tank and Mike, the two biggest guys, chose teams. We had enough kids for four on each side. Gramps got chosen first by Tank, who then picked Tony. As the new guy around, I got chosen last and wound up on Mike's team.

Tony pointed out the bases—a sewer, a fire hydrant, and a manhole cover. Another manhole cover was home plate. Tank's little brother was lookout. He had to watch for cars.

It wasn't anything like softball. The bat was a sawed-off mop handle, and the ball was a pink Spalding. Because there was no pitcher, the hitter bounced the ball himself. He got three swings at the ball, that was all.

First time at bat, Gramps hit a ground ball and rounded the bases before the ball was even picked up.

I covered first and second base, and dropped a few balls and missed some others. No one seemed to care much. It was fun just to shout and cheer and yell as the light faded and the pavement cooled off.

"Car coming!" Tank's little brother shouted every once in a while.

The game would stop until the car rolled by, and then pick up again. Later, the cars seemed to disappear, and Tank's little brother sat down on the curb and fell asleep.

By then it was almost dark. I had to concentrate on the ball to even see it. I was on the third base sewer, ready to run home. Mike hit a ground ball that bounced against the far curb and veered in my direction. I could just make out the ball as it headed toward the center of the street.

Gramps ran out, watching the ball, ready to grab it. A horn blew, and out of the corner of my eye I saw a car.

"Car coming!" I shouted to Gramps.

He stopped, and a DeSoto rumbled by.

"Thanks, Sam!" Gramps called, loping off to retrieve the ball.

That night I stretched out on top of the sheets. I hung my leg over the side of the bed so I could rub Red's back with my foot. He sighed and started snoring.

I listened to the Brooklyn sounds coming through the window. It wasn't West Virginia, that was for sure. I still wasn't too good at dealing with anything new. But I was getting better. And Mom was happy. She didn't seem so different anymore.

Some things about Brooklyn were even "great": Mom's job, and the ocean, and fishing, and Tony, and Gramps. I started to sing "The Star-Spangled Banner." Before I got to the word "home," I was asleep.